P9-DWO-613

Capitol Hill Library

JUL 16 2019

Star tripped over a thick vine and Ava gasped as a creeper snagged around her arm, almost pulling her from Star's back. She wrenched her arm free. "Star!" she exclaimed. "These plants must be enchanted!"

LOOK OUT FOR MORE ADVENTURES AT

UNICORN ACADEMY

Sophia and Rainbow

Scarlett and Blaze

Ava and Star

Isabel and Cloud

Layla and Dancer

Olivia and Snowflake

★ ★ ★

UNICORN ACADEMY
Ava and Star

JULIE SYKES
illustrated by LUCY TRUMAN

A STEPPING STONE BOOK™
Random House 🏠 New York

To Eleanor Jones, who loves to write magical stories too!

This is a work of fiction. Names, characters, places, and incidents either are the product of the author's imagination or are used fictitiously. Any resemblance to actual persons, living or dead, events, or locales is entirely coincidental.

Text copyright © 2018 by Julie Sykes and Linda Chapman
Cover art and interior illustrations copyright © 2018 by Lucy Truman

All rights reserved. Published in the United States by Random House Children's Books, a division of Penguin Random House LLC, New York. Originally published in paperback by Nosy Crow Ltd, London, in 2018.

Random House and the colophon are registered trademarks and A Stepping Stone Book and the colophon are trademarks of Penguin Random House LLC.

Visit us on the Web! rhcbooks.com

Educators and librarians, for a variety of teaching tools,
visit us at RHTeachersLibrarians.com

Library of Congress Cataloging-in-Publication Data
Names: Sykes, Julie, author. | Truman, Lucy, illustrator.
Title: Ava and Star / Julie Sykes; illustrated by Lucy Truman.
Description: First American edition. | New York: Random House, [2019] |
Series: Unicorn Academy; #3 | Originally published: London: Nosy Crow, 2018.
Summary: "When the sky berries that unicorns need to survive disappear, Ava
and her unicorn, Star, must find more special berries before every unicorn's
magic fades away"—Provided by publisher.
Identifiers: LCCN 2018034606 | ISBN 978-1-9848-5088-1 (pbk.) |
ISBN 978-1-9848-5089-8 (hardcover library binding) |
ISBN 978-1-9848-5090-4 (ebook)
Subjects: | CYAC: Unicorns—Fiction. | Magic—Fiction. | Friendship—
Fiction. | Boarding schools—Fiction. | Schools—Fiction.
Classification: LCC PZ7.S98325 Av 2019 | DDC [E]—dc23

Printed in the United States of America
10 9 8 7 6 5 4 3 2 1
First American Edition

Random House Children's Books supports the First Amendment
and celebrates the right to read.

CHAPTER 1

"Star, wake up," whispered Ava.

Star was asleep in her stable. She looked so sweet, with her eyes shut tight and her yellow-and-purple mane curling over her white coat. Ava smoothed a lilac curl that was sticking up around Star's spiraled gold-and-purple horn.

"Ava?" Star's eyes snapped open and she scrambled to her hooves. "It's early, even for you. Is something wrong?"

Ava grinned. "No, everything's fine. I'm just excited! Last night the teachers told us we're going on a scavenger hunt this morning instead of lessons. We've got to collect things from around the school grounds in teams!"

Star pricked up her ears. "That sounds fun!"

Ava nodded. "I woke up thinking about it, and when I looked out the window, I saw something I had to show you. Come with me!"

Blinking and yawning, Star followed Ava through the stable of sleeping unicorns to the door.

Ava stopped. "Close your eyes."

Star obediently shut her eyes. Ava felt her heart swell with happiness as she realized how much her unicorn trusted her. Putting her hand on Star's warm neck, she guided her outside.

"You can open them now," she whispered. "Look!"

"Wow!" Star blinked. A ball of sunshine was visible on the horizon. As it rose, filling the gap between two mountains, the dark sky rippled with orange, pink, and gold.

"Doesn't the school look beautiful?" said Ava. Across the lawn, the marble walls and glass windows of Unicorn Academy glowed in the sunrise, and in the distance the multicolored water of Sparkle Lake glittered and shone.

"It's the best sunrise I've seen in ages," said Star.

Ava smiled. "I had to share it with you. Spring's coming, Star. I can smell it in the air! Shall we plant my new seedlings before I have to go for breakfast?"

"Good plan!" said Star eagerly. "I'll dig the holes."

"That would be brilliant." Ava kissed her unicorn on the purple star on her forehead. "I love having you as my unicorn. I can't imagine being partnered with a unicorn who didn't like gardening!"

"And I can't imagine being partnered with a girl who didn't like nature!" said Star, her warm breath tickling Ava and making her giggle.

Ava and Star had been paired together in January, three months ago, when they'd both started at Unicorn Academy. Ava still found it hard to believe that she was really here, training to become a guardian of wonderful Unicorn Island.

The island was nourished by magical waters that flowed up from the center of the earth and out through the fountain in Sparkle Lake. Rivers carried the precious water around the land so that it helped all the people, animals, and plants on Unicorn Island to flourish.

Students usually spent a year at Unicorn Academy when they were ten, but sometimes they stayed longer if their unicorn needed more time to discover their magic power or if they hadn't yet bonded with their unicorn. Bonding was the highest form of friendship, and when it happened, a lock of the student's hair would turn the same color as their unicorn's mane. Ava couldn't help feeling a little surprised she and Star hadn't bonded already.

"Do you think Ms. Primrose paired us together because we both love plants and nature?" asked Star.

"Maybe," said Ava. "Or maybe there was another reason. You never know with Ms. Primrose."

Ms. Primrose was the wise head teacher who had been in charge of the academy for many years. She was strict, but she could also be very kind.

"Well, whatever her reason, I'm glad she did," said Star. "I wonder when I'll find out what my magic power is and when we'll bond."

Ava felt a clench in her stomach. Two of the girls from Sapphire dorm had already bonded with their unicorns. Ava couldn't help but worry that she was doing something wrong. She knew a lot about plants and animals, but she wasn't very good at reading and writing. What if Star never found her magic power and they never bonded because she wasn't clever enough to help her? That would be awful!

Star nudged her. "Should we get your plants from the greenhouse?"

6

Ava squashed her growing anxiety. "Aren't you forgetting something?" she said. "You haven't had any breakfast yet!"

Star burst out laughing. "Silly me, I'm getting as forgetful as you, Ava!"

"Impossible!" Ava chuckled.

She and Star went back inside the stables. Ava found a bucket and went to fill it with sky berries. But when she lifted the lid of the feed bin, she blinked in surprise.

"It's almost empty!" she said to Star, who was watching from the doorway. She checked the other feed bins. "They all are."

"What? They

can't be. The gardeners fill the bins with berries every day," said Star.

Sky berries grew on the mountain slopes behind the school. Not only were they the unicorns' favorite food, but the berries were full of the vitamins they needed to stay healthy and helped keep the unicorns' magic strong.

Star came over to check, but as she put her nose into a feed bin, she knocked it over. The remaining berries spilled onto the floor.

"Star!" exclaimed Ava.

"Whoops!" said Star, nudging the berries into a pile with her muzzle. "I'm sorry, Ava."

"Don't worry." Ava scooped them up and put them back into the bin. She adored Star, but sometimes she wished she weren't quite so clumsy. "There are only enough berries for the unicorns to have breakfast. I'd better tell Ms. Rosemary." Ms. Rosemary, the Care of Unicorns teacher, was in charge of the stables. "Now, eat up," she said, filling Star's bucket with berries.

Star gobbled up her berries. As she finished her last mouthful, she gave Ava a hopeful look. "Is there still time to plant your new seedlings before your breakfast?"

"If we're quick," said Ava.

First Ava and Star went to the potting shed to collect their gardening tools, then to the greenhouse for Ava's plants. Between them they carried everything to Ava's small patch of garden.

The spring earth was soft and easy to dig. Star made the holes, while Ava rescued the worms that got dug up, carefully moving them to a new home. Then Ava placed each seedling into a hole and patted earth around it. Star leaned over her shoulder. The last seedling was smaller than the rest. Star accidentally nudged it with her nose and it fell over.

Puff! A tiny spark flickered next to the plant.

"Oh!" exclaimed Ava.

"Sorry, I was being clumsy again," said Star anxiously. "I didn't do any damage, did I?"

"I meant the spark." Ava sniffed the air. "And what's that sweet smell?"

"What smell?" Star looked mystified.

"It's gone now, but it smelled like . . ." Ava shook her head. "Nothing, I probably imagined it. For a second I thought you were getting your magic, though. Wouldn't it be brilliant if you had plant magic? Imagine what fun we could have."

Every unicorn had a special type of magic. In Sapphire dorm, Sophia's unicorn had light magic and Scarlett's unicorn had fire magic.

Star stared at Ava. "Plant magic is very powerful. I'm much too clumsy to have something that special."

"Being clumsy doesn't matter. I bet you could have plant magic!" Ava dusted the dirt from her hands and then stroked Star's forehead. "Why don't you try again?"

Star dipped her head and blew on the ground. Nothing happened. She gently touched the row of seedlings with her nose, taking extra care not to knock them over.

"Nothing," she said sadly. "They're exactly the same size. I knew I wouldn't have plant magic."

"You still might!" Ava hugged her tightly. "And anyway, I love you just the way you are, whatever magic you end up having."

Star whinnied happily.

Just then there was the sound of someone approaching at a fast gallop. Ava looked around and saw her best friend, Sophia, racing up to them on her handsome unicorn, Rainbow.

"Sophia! You look like you're in a hurry!" exclaimed Ava.

"I am," panted Sophia, her dark curls bouncing on her shoulders as Rainbow halted. "You need to come with me. Ms. Rosemary wants us all to meet at Sparkle Lake. We're about to start the scavenger hunt!"

"But what about breakfast?" said Ava.

"We're taking it with us in backpacks."

"Really?" said Ava. "You're not joking?"

"Cross my heart it's true," said Sophia, folding her arms over her hoodie. "Ms. Primrose wants us to find the things on the scavenger hunt list as quickly as possible!"

"What's the rush?" said Ava.

"I don't know." Sophia's eyes shone. "But isn't it exciting? Let's go to the lake!"

CHAPTER 2

Ava and Sophia joined the noisy group of students and unicorns gathering along the shore of Sparkle Lake. The colorful fountain and waters of the lake looked extra glittery in the spring sunlight.

"Ava, Sophia, over here!" called Scarlett eagerly.

Star and Rainbow threaded their way through the crowd to where Scarlett and two of their other friends from Sapphire dormitory—Isabel and Layla—were gathered with their unicorns.

"This scavenger hunt is going to be way more fun than boring old lessons!" said Isabel, grinning. "The first team back wins a prize."

"I wonder why we have to leave so quickly?" said Ava. "It's a bit odd, isn't it?"

Layla looked anxious. "I hope everything's okay," she said. "Lessons are never normally just canceled."

"Billy told me it's because the teachers are all having a meeting," said Sophia.

"What about?" said Scarlett.

"Maybe it has to do with the lake," suggested Sophia. "After all, someone's already attacked it twice. Maybe someone's trying to harm it again?"

"Oh, I hope not!" said Layla.

A chill swept through Ava. In the short time she'd been at Unicorn Academy, a mysterious person had tampered with Sparkle Lake on two different occasions. The first time, the lake had been polluted so that the unicorns couldn't drink its magical waters. The second time, a freezing spell had turned the fountain and the lake to solid ice. She peered at the magical multicolored water, trying to see if it looked different from usual.

"Stop being such worrywarts, all of you!" said Isabel impatiently. "I'm sure Ms. Primrose won't let anything happen to the lake again. We should be concentrating on the important things—like getting into teams. We're supposed to be in twos or threes."

Sophia slipped her arm through Ava's. "We're a team."

"Definitely!" declared Ava. She and Sophia had met on their very first day at Unicorn Academy and had been friends ever since. Star and Rainbow bumped noses. They were best friends, too!

"You'll come with me and Scarlett, won't you, Layla?" Isabel said quickly. Layla was one of the smartest students at the academy. She spent a lot of her time in the library.

Layla looked pleased to be asked. "Okay!"

The noise and chatter rose as everyone sorted out their teams. Billy and Jack high-fived their friend Jason, while Jacinta and Delia fawned over Valentina, who was looking as smart as ever in expensive riding clothes and shiny boots. Valentina's aunt was the strict Geography and Culture teacher, Ms. Nettles, and her wealthy parents were school trustees—a fact Valentina never let anyone forget.

"Where's Olivia?" said Ava, her eyes scanning the crowd for the other member of Sapphire dorm. "Look, there she is with Snowflake."

Olivia and Snowflake were at the water's edge. As usual, redheaded Olivia was smiling, but Ava noticed something sad about her eyes. *She looks a bit lonely,* she thought.

"Olivia doesn't have a best friend, does she?" she said to Sophia.

Sophia looked surprised. "No, but she gets along so well with everyone. I don't think she minds being on her own."

"I'm not so sure," Ava said thoughtfully. "I can't imagine what I'd do if I didn't have you to share my secrets with. I tell you everything."

"Me too! You know all my secrets," said Sophia with a smile. "Well, you and Rainbow."

Ava looked across at Olivia again. "Let's ask her to join us."

"Sure. Hey, Olivia!" Sophia called, waving at her. "Would you like to join our team?"

A huge smile lit up Olivia's face. "Yes, please,"

she said, bringing Snowflake, her beautiful white-and-silver unicorn, over to join them. Ava smiled as she approached, realizing that although they'd been sharing a dorm for three months, she still didn't really know much about Olivia. She was a very good listener, but she didn't talk about herself or her family much. *Sophia and I should try to include her more,* Ava thought.

Just then a woman riding a tall, slender unicorn with a deep-pink mane and tail came cantering across the lawn toward them. It was Ms. Rosemary and her unicorn, Blossom.

Blossom reached the lake and stamped her hoof. The girls, boys, and their unicorns stopped chatting and turned to face her and the teacher.

"Thank you for coming so quickly," said Ms. Rosemary. Her eyes twinkled as she looked around at their excited faces. "As you have heard, there's been a change to the timetable today. Lessons are temporarily suspended, and while the staff attend a meeting, I hope you'll all enjoy going on a scavenger hunt!"

Jason, a tall boy with curly black hair, called out, "What's the meeting about, Miss? It must be important if you're letting us out of class."

A few people giggled, and even Ms. Rosemary smiled.

"It *is* important, but it's nothing to worry about," she said. "Anyway, enough about boring meetings. Pass these around please, dears." She handed a stack of pink paper and a pile of backpacks to Ava's group. "One bag and one list to each team, please. There is food in the bags, and you can store the items you collect in there too."

The students buzzed with excitement as Ava and her friends handed everything out. Ava caught bits of ideas as the list was discussed. She couldn't wait to figure out where to find the items.

"That's it," said Sophia at last. "This list and bag must be ours."

"Thank you, girls," said Ms. Rosemary. Raising her voice, she called for everyone to listen.

"Remember, the scavenger hunt is more than just a race. It's about teamwork and using your combined knowledge to find the exact items listed. Now, are you all ready to begin? On the count of five . . ."

The whole school joined in, counting down with Ms. Rosemary, "Five, four, three, two, one . . . GO!"

There was a huge cheer as the unicorns and

their riders galloped away in different directions, leaving Ava, Sophia, and Olivia still deciding where to start.

"Not fair!" said Ava, waving the list. "They got a head start. We haven't had a chance to look yet."

"We'll soon catch up," said Olivia. "What's on the list, Ava?"

Ava's stomach tightened as she looked down at the list. Oh no. How had she ended up as the one reading it aloud? Reading in her head was hard enough, but reading to an audience was almost impossible. The words seemed to jump around and her brain seemed to freeze. She swallowed and stared at the sparkly purple writing on the sheet of pink paper.

"A f-f—"

"Quickly, Ava!" urged Olivia. "We need to get going!"

Ava bit her lip. The purple sparkly writing

was even harder to read than a book. The words might as well have been enchanted, the way they were wriggling about! Why wouldn't they stay still long enough for her to work out what they said?

Sophia plucked the list out of her hands. "Can I do the reading, Ava? Pleeease?" she begged. "Please let me!"

Ava gave her a grateful smile. "Okay."

Sophia was the only person Ava had told about her embarrassing secret, and she was glad she had. Sophia often tried to help without letting on to the others. She also kept insisting that Ava had nothing to be ashamed about, but Ava knew that was just because she was such a good friend. Her clever older brother and sister often teased her for being slow.

"A feather from a snowy owl, a twig of conkhorn, a sprig of knitbone, two blue stones, two heart-shaped berries, a jumping bean, and some fox fur." Sophia looked up in dismay. "I don't know where to find any of these."

Olivia looked mystified. "Knitbone? Is that even a real thing? It sounds made up!"

"Knitbone's an herb," said Ava, smiling in relief. Not only had she heard of every single thing on the list, but she had a good idea where

they could find them all. "I'm growing knitbone in my garden. Let's go there first."

"Lead on, clever boots!" said Sophia.

Ava buried her hands in Star's mane, and they took the lead, racing to her garden, with Sophia and Rainbow and Olivia and Snowflake galloping close behind. The scavenger hunt had begun!

CHAPTER 3

"Ava, this is brilliant." Olivia stared at the neat rows of seedlings that Ava and Star had planted that morning. Ava's plot in the kitchen gardens was laid out in sections, with a flower bed tucked away in a corner and sheltered on two sides by a red-brick wall.

"It's not up to much right now," Ava apologized, gesturing around her plot. "Most of the plants look dead, but they're not. They're sleeping. They'll start flowering when the air and ground warm up some more."

"I think it's awesome," said Sophia loyally. "Which one is knitbone?"

"That's here." Ava jumped from Star and carefully walked between two rows of herbs. She stopped at a pale-green plant with spiky leaves in the shape of a fish bone and carefully removed a sprig. "Knitbone has tiny red flowers in the spring. Look here, you can just see the buds. You have to be careful not to confuse it with boneheal—it's very similar but with feathery leaves."

"You're so clever to know so much," said Olivia, studying the knitbone cutting.

Ava let a wing of dark hair fall across her face to hide her embarrassment as she stored the knitbone in the backpack. Olivia couldn't be more wrong. She definitely wasn't clever. "I like plants, so I guess it's easy for me to remember stuff about them. What else do we need to find?"

Sophia read the list again.

"There's a snowy owl nest in the orchard," Ava said. "Let's go there next."

"I'm hungry," said Sophia. She rummaged in the bag and found some delicious breakfast pastries. "Let's eat these as we go!"

They set off, munching on the cinnamon and apple pastries. Soon, thanks to Ava's knowledge of the plants and animals at the academy, they had collected a snowy owl feather, a twig of conkhorn, and two blue stones. Then she suggested they look for fox fur near the boat swing on the playground. "I go there to think sometimes, and I've seen the foxes there, especially at dusk when the cubs come out to play."

They raced to the playground. "You're right. Here's some fur!" exclaimed Olivia as she pulled a snagged piece of fox fur from the boat swing. "I'm very glad we have you, Ava."

"Yes, you're so smart. You definitely know more about plants and wildlife than anyone else at the school," said Sophia.

Ava chuckled to hide her blushes. Her friends were lovely even if they were wrong. "Stop it, you two. My head's getting so big it's not going to fit through the door when I get back to school." She frowned. "Hang on. What's that noise? It sounds like someone screaming!"

They all listened. There were definitely screams coming from a little way off in a grove of trees.

"Quick! Someone must be in trouble!" Sophia said, urging Rainbow into a fast canter.

The unicorns thundered along the path and into the trees. They skidded to a halt as they saw Valentina, her back to a tree, screeching and waving a stick around while her friends, Delia and Jacinta, clung to each other on the path.

"It's going to eat me!" Valentina was crying.

Golden Briar, Valentina's unicorn, saw Ava and the others. "Help!" he whinnied. "Please help!"

Ava felt a shiver of fear. What was going on?

Jacinta's and Delia's unicorns collided on the path as they snorted and pranced around.

"What is it?" asked Sophia, scanning the area frantically. "What's going to eat you?"

"That . . . that . . . sp . . . sp . . . !" The words stuck in Valentina's throat. "SPIDER!" she choked out, pointing in front of her.

"Spider?" echoed Ava. She hurried forward, her eyes widening as she spotted a plump spider, the size of an apple, just in front of Valentina. It had long legs and googly eyes and was the hairiest spider Ava had ever seen. It scuttled a few steps closer to Valentina, its huge eyes full of hope.

"Help!" Valentina turned whiter than a snowy-owl feather. "I want Mooooommy!" she screamed.

The spider scuttled closer, and Valentina took aim, hurling a stick at it.

"Stop!" shouted Ava. "It's not dangerous!"

Luckily, Valentina missed. The terrified spider leaped past her and scuttled up a tree.

"NEVER do that again!" Ava stormed over to Valentina. "Do not EVER hurt a spider or any creature. Not unless it attacks you. That's a cave spider. They're quite harmless."

"Harmless?" Valentina repeated, the color returning to her cheeks as she backed hastily away from the tree.

Ava nodded. "Cave spiders live underground and usually only come out at night. This one must be lost." She picked up Valentina's stick, snapped it in half, and threw the pieces under a bush. "I can't believe you did that," she continued hotly. "You scared the poor thing so much it's run up into a tree. What are we going to do? If we leave it there, it might get eaten by a bird."

"Like I care!" exclaimed Valentina. "Stupid spider! I hope it does get eaten, frightening me like that."

"I think you frightened it more," said Sophia.

Olivia burst out laughing, and even Jacinta and Delia giggled.

Valentina rounded on them. "What are you two laughing at? You screamed too. You're both useless. Give that to me. What's next to find?"

Valentina snatched the list from Jacinta and then rode off, with her friends jumping on their unicorns and trotting after her.

Ava didn't hesitate. She didn't like climbing much, but she had to help the spider. Asking Star to move as close to the tree as possible, she clambered onto the lowest branch. She sat for a moment, trying to work out how best to climb the tree and rescue the spider that was now sitting on a higher branch.

"Careful, Ava," called Olivia anxiously.

Ava climbed up slowly. "Hello there," she whispered. "Who's a lovely spider? That's right. I'm not going to hurt you."

The branch bowed as Ava started to slide slowly along it.

"Ava!" Sophia warned. "You're really high up."

A gust of wind rocked the branches. Ava froze, clinging on tightly until the tree stilled. The spider clung on too, its hairy body shaking so violently that its googly eyes disappeared under long hair. Seeing the spider's fear gave Ava extra courage. She murmured soothingly to it. The spider peeped from under its fringe and tentatively stretched out one long leg. Ava held her breath. Warily, the spider reached out a second leg. Ava forgot about the scavenger hunt, fascinated by the spider's large, expressive eyes. But then there was a sudden rush of air. A wing brushed Ava's face, and a falcon swooped down, its curved beak open as it dived at the spider.

"No! Get off!" Ava batted the bird away. There was an indignant squawk, and then she lost her balance. With a gasp, she started to fall. . . .

35

Twisting desperately, Ava grabbed at the branch, the bark biting into her hands as she caught hold. She hung from the tree, legs dangling.

"Ava!" squeaked Sophia and Olivia.

"I'm right beneath you, Ava," called Star.

Ava's arms ached, but she hung on tightly until the branch stopped swaying. Knowing Star was standing beneath her made her feel braver, and she prepared to pull herself back up. It was a bit of a scramble, but at last she was sitting astride the branch again.

"Well done!" Sophia called in relief.

"Thanks," panted Ava, blowing on her stinging fingers.

This time, when Ava offered the spider her hand, it came at once, scuttling into her palm. Ava giggled as its little feet tickled her. Gently, she stroked its back. "Look at you, so cute!"

The spider gazed at her adoringly, then it rubbed its head against her hand and shook its bottom like a happy dog.

"Aww!" cooed Ava. "You're gorgeous. Valentina is a total fluff head!" she called to the others. "Cave spiders are the friendliest spiders ever. This one's definitely lost. Sorry, you two, but I can't go on with the scavenger hunt until I've found its cave. I'll catch up with you later."

"We're not going anywhere without you," said Sophia. "Where do you think it lives?"

"There are some caves a bit farther on through

the trees, aren't there, Ava?" called Star. "We went there once when we were looking for shadow-vetch seeds for your garden."

"Good thinking!" Holding the spider carefully, Ava slowly climbed down and got back on Star. "Can you take us there, please?"

Star whinnied. "Of course!"

They set off through the trees until they reached a rocky cliff face. The spider perked up as they got closer, dancing in Ava's hand, its long legs kicking wildly.

Ava couldn't stop giggling. "Is this your home, then? Is that what you're trying to tell me?"

In answer, the spider jumped onto Star's back, let out a sparkly pink thread, then used it to sail down to the ground. It scuttled across the grass and into a small cave in the side of the cliff. Ava sighed happily. There was a rustle, and the spider's head popped out of the entrance, its big eyes wobbling. It waved a leg at Ava and Star before disappearing again, this time for good.

Ava smiled and hugged Star. "I love a happy ending."

"Me too!" Sophia agreed. "But we haven't finished yet. Where's that list?" She pulled it out of her jodhpurs pocket, laid it on Rainbow's neck, and smoothed out the creases. "We need heart-shaped berries and also a jumping bean. Ava, any ideas?"

Ava grinned. "Actually, yes. Follow me. . . ."

When every item on the list had been scavenged and safely stored in the backpack, Ava, Sophia, and Olivia raced back to school.

Olivia was confident that they'd won. "And all thanks to Ava."

Ava wasn't so sure. She wasn't surprised when they saw that Scarlett's team had beaten them back to school. As they rode up to the finish line, Scarlett and Isabel were triumphantly hugging a rather scared-looking Layla. Ava felt sorry for her. Layla was very clever, but Ava was sure that she didn't enjoy galloping as much as everyone else. She gave her a sympathetic smile.

"We won!" Isabel boasted loudly.

"You did not win!" Ms. Nettles was in charge of checking the bags of scavenged items. She gave a thin smile, her glasses rattling on her bony nose as

she held up a plant. "This is boneheal. You were asked to find knitbone."

Isabel scowled. "What? Are you sure? The flowers . . ."

"The red flowers are similar to knitbone, but the leaves are quite different." Ms. Nettles took Ava's bag and pulled out the contents one by one, checking them off her list. "Lovely," she said. "What a fine specimen of knitbone. You must tell me where you found this herb."

"I . . . I . . . grew it," Ava stammered, the intensity of Ms. Nettles's stare making her uncomfortable.

"Really." Ms. Nettles looked thoughtful.

Ava looked away, and when she glanced back Ms. Nettles was continuing to empty the bag.

"Well done, girls," she said. Her sour face crinkled into a rare smile. "You are the winners! Your prize is a giant bar of chocolate. Don't eat it all before lunch!"

"I can't believe it! I never win at anything," said Olivia as they rode their unicorns back to the stables. "Thanks for letting me join your team. I've had so much fun."

It didn't take long to settle the unicorns with a deep bed of fresh straw and an apple and carrot snack. Ava left Star drinking from her water trough, which automatically refilled with colorful water from the lake, before leaving the stables with Sophia and Olivia.

"I'm starving," said Sophia. "I hope there's something good for lunch."

Lunch was a huge buffet with sandwiches, tapas, pizza, and spring rolls. Ava and her friends ate hungrily, sitting at a table overlooking the lake with all their friends from Sapphire dorm. Isabel was still a little huffy over losing the scavenger hunt, but her smile returned as she plowed

through a multicolored ice-cream sundae with cherries for dessert.

Lessons started again after lunch. Ava's class had Care of Unicorns with Ms. Rosemary. Ava was surprised how distracted their teacher was.

Instead of welcoming them, she stood at the window, gazing out at the mountains. When everyone was seated, Scarlett had to cough three times to get her attention. Ms. Rosemary turned and stared at the class as if she couldn't work out how they'd gotten there.

Ava was expecting Ms. Rosemary to finish the lesson on hoof care that they'd started yesterday, but instead she gave them back the items they had scavenged that morning and told them to lay them out on the desks and write about them. She then started to leaf through a pile of books.

Ava was eager to write all about the things they had gathered in the scavenger hunt, but it wasn't that easy. The words were in her head, but she couldn't get them down on the page quickly enough or spell them correctly. Soon her brain was aching with frustration. Sighing, she looked

up and saw Ms. Rosemary running a hand through her hair.

"No, that won't help because it's not a full moon . . . nor that because it's not summer . . . ," the teacher muttered to herself. "There must be a potion in here somewhere that will work."

Ava twiddled her pencil. It sounded like Ms. Rosemary was looking for a spell. But to do what? Ava started to worry about the lake. Could someone be trying to harm it again?

Her eyes flashed. The unicorns needed the lake water. If someone was trying to sabotage it, then she and her friends would stop them—no matter what!

CHAPTER 5

Ms. Rosemary suddenly stood up. She had a small book in her hand and she looked excited. "Right, everyone, I need to take the finest specimen of each item collected to Ms. Primrose."

"Why?" asked Jack.

"Ms. Primrose is going to make a potion to help with a small problem we have at school. It's nothing for you to worry about!" Ms. Rosemary said. She walked around, taking a selection of the items. Finally, she picked up the knitbone and feather that Ava's team had collected. "Perfect! Get on with your work, please, while I go to see

Ms. Primrose. I expect you all to have finished when I return."

The moment Ms. Rosemary left, everyone started talking.

"What's going on?" said Scarlett.

"Yes, what's this problem Ms. Rosemary's talking about?" Isabel said. "Why do the teachers need a potion?"

"Maybe it's about the lake again," called Jason.

The noise level in the room rose.

"Shh!" said Olivia. "We'll get into trouble. We need to finish our work." They settled down again, still talking but in quieter voices. Ava glanced around at everyone scribbling hard.

Valentina, stopping to stretch her fingers, caught Ava's eye. Ava looked away, but Valentina was already nudging Jacinta and Delia. "Ava's hardly written a thing. And she spelled *Scavenger*

Hunt wrong, even though it's on the board. Silly girl!"

Olivia's head whipped up. "Leave Ava alone!" she hissed. "She's much smarter than you, Valentina. She knows a ton about animals, including spiders."

"Yes, she does," chipped in Sophia. "What was that dangerous creature you found today, Valentina? Oh, that's right, a harmless cave spider!"

Valentina turned bright red. "Oh, for goodness' sake, don't you care that Ava can't spell?"

"We care that you were making fun of her, which isn't very nice," said Sophia, and Olivia agreed.

"Leave Ava alone," added Scarlett. The rest of Sapphire dorm all glared at Valentina.

Valentina turned from red to purple. She glanced over at Jacinta and Delia, but they kept their heads bent. With an angry sigh, Valentina went back to her work.

Ava gave her friends a warm smile, but inside she was frozen with shame. Valentina had called her a silly girl, and that's exactly how she felt. Why couldn't she have even half the brains of her friends or her older brother and sister? Ava barely wrote a thing after that. She felt too miserable.

After a while, Ms. Rosemary came back into the classroom. She looked gloomy.

"Did you manage to find Ms. Primrose, Miss? Did she make a potion?" asked Billy.

"Yes," said Ms. Rosemary with a sigh. "But it didn't work. We'll have to try something else. Now, hand your notes in, please, so I can see what you've been doing."

"Not much in YOUR case," Valentina whispered to Ava as she brushed past her to hand her notes in. Ava blushed hotly.

The instant the lesson ended, she raced to the stable and told Star what Valentina had said. The unicorn listened carefully.

"Valentina is wrong!" she exclaimed. "You're not a silly girl. How could you be when you know so much about nature?"

"That's easy stuff. Anyone can learn about that," said Ava miserably.

Star nuzzled Ava. "I don't think they can. Your memory for plants is amazing, Ava, and you're kind and generous and everyone likes you."

Ava's cheeks warmed. To cover her embarrassment, she backed away. "Um . . . thanks," she muttered. She could hear the others arriving and starting to collect the feed buckets for the unicorns' dinner. "Let me go and get you some sky berries."

Ava's heart was lighter, and she swung the bucket as she entered the feed room. Star always knew what to say to cheer her up. She realized she hadn't told her about Ms. Rosemary's strange behavior and the potion the teachers wanted to make. *I'll tell her while she's eating*, she thought.

Ava dumped the bucket on the floor, lifted the feed-bin lid, and groaned. There were hardly any sky berries left, certainly not enough for every unicorn in the stable to have an evening meal. She'd meant to tell Ms. Rosemary that morning, but she'd forgotten. Guilt flashed through her.

The unicorns won't be able to have berries for supper tonight, and it's all my fault, she thought.

The rest of Sapphire dorm came into the feed room. "Scoot over, Ava," said Isabel. "What's wrong? You look upset."

Ava bit her lip. "We're almost out of sky berries. There's not enough to go around."

"Let's volunteer to collect some more," Layla suggested.

Ava nodded. "The bushes grow on the lower slopes of the mountain, just behind the school," she said. "If we all go, we'll soon pick enough for tonight's feed."

"I'll help," said Sophia.

"Me too," said Olivia.

Just then, Ms. Rosemary swept into the feed room. Locks of brown hair escaped from the silver clips she wore, and, unusual for her, she was frowning.

"Listen, please," she said, clapping her hands to get everyone's attention. "As you can see, we have a serious sky-berry shortage. There are none left on the bushes on the lower mountain slopes where we usually gather them. Hopefully the problem is temporary, but until we work out a solution, sky berries will have to be rationed."

Ava frowned. Sky berries were easy to grow. The faster you picked them, the faster new ones appeared. "Why aren't there any on the bushes?" she asked.

"We don't know, Ava." Ms. Rosemary sighed. "The sky-berry bushes were fine yesterday morning, but by the evening we noticed they'd started to wilt. The stable staff spent half the night watering them with

magical water from the lake, but when I went to check on them shortly after dawn, every single bush had shriveled and there were no berries left on the branches at all."

"But that's not possible," said Ava. Even if the sky-berry bushes had wilted, the water from Sparkle Lake should have made things right again.

"It is very unusual," said Ms. Rosemary. "Ms. Primrose and Sage made a potion to help, but it didn't work." Ms. Rosemary shook her head. "We don't know what's going on."

Seeing the worry in her eyes, a shiver ran through Ava. Was someone trying to harm the academy and the unicorns again—not the lake this time but by destroying the sky berries with dark magic?

"There must be other sky-berry bushes in the mountains," said Sophia.

Ava nodded. "We could go and look on the higher slopes."

"Can we, Miss?" Olivia said eagerly.

"I'm sorry, girls," said Ms. Rosemary. "But Ms. Primrose and Sage have searched the high mountains and didn't find one sky-berry bush with fruit."

More students were crowding into the feed room. Raising her voice, Ms. Rosemary addressed everyone. "Sky berries are rationed to one small handful a day until further notice. Unfortunately, without a good diet of sky berries, your unicorns will grow weaker, so from now on unicorns must stay inside to conserve their energy. Unicorn magic is also banned, unless there's an emergency."

Sophia stared. "Magic is banned?" she echoed.

Ms. Rosemary looked grim. "That's an order from Ms. Primrose, and it must be obeyed!"

55

Star was very understanding when she saw the tiny portion of sky berries mixed into her feed. "I'm sure it won't be for long," she said. "Ms. Primrose and Sage will fix the problem."

Ava hardly ate anything at dinner. She kept thinking of how Star had eaten her meal that evening, chewing her food slowly, making every mouthful of the sky berries last. It made Ava feel guilty about the huge amount of food available to her. From the subdued atmosphere, Ava sensed that most students felt the same way. Everyone spoke in whispers, and the delicious food was only picked at.

After dinner, Sapphire dorm usually hung out in their lounge to play games, listen to music, and chat. Ava didn't have the heart for it. After a quick visit to the stable to say good night to Star, she went to bed. Her dorm-mates joined her.

"No riding tomorrow," said Isabel glumly.

"We're going to miss our cross-country jumping lesson," Scarlett said. "Blaze and I were really looking forward to it."

"I hope the unicorns will be all right. What if they get sick because they don't have enough sky berries to eat?" Layla worried. "I'll braid Dancer's mane and tail tomorrow. I hope that cheers him up."

Ava lay in bed, staring at a patch of moonlight shining on the ceiling. Thoughts whizzed around

her head until she thought it might explode. Ms. Primrose was the wisest person she knew. She never made mistakes, but she had to be wrong this time. The mountain range was huge. Ms. Primrose couldn't have checked the whole thing in one day. The more Ava thought about it, the more convinced she was that there had to be healthy sky-berry bushes growing somewhere.

A little after sunrise, Ava gave up trying to sleep. Quietly, she got up, dressed in jodhpurs and her favorite lilac hoodie, and then headed to the stables. Passing the lake, Ava heard someone calling her name.

"Sophia!" Ava waited for her friend to catch up. "Why are you up so early?"

"I couldn't sleep."

"Me neither." Ava stared at the multicolored lake, its waters glittering with a fiery glow in the sunrise. "I'm sure there have to be sky berries somewhere in the mountains. If only we knew where to look."

"Rainbow might be able to help," Sophia said slowly. "His magic lets him see things that are in other places, so he might be able to show us where there are some healthy bushes."

"That's a brilliant idea. Let's ask him," said Ava.

"But we can't." Sophia's face crumpled. "Ms. Rosemary banned the unicorns from doing magic, remember."

"Unless it's an emergency," Ava said slowly.

Her eyes met Sophia's.

"This is an emergency," said Sophia, nodding.

"It really is," said Ava. "Our unicorns need sky berries to stay healthy and magical, and Unicorn Island needs our unicorns!" Ava spoke passionately, pushing the hair back from her face and almost crushing the sprig of blue forget-me-not that she always wore in it.

"You're right," said Sophia. "Let's ask Rainbow to help."

Ava and Sophia ran to the stables and found Rainbow taking a long drink from his trough. He turned to face Sophia, multicolored water droplets spinning through the air as he shook his head in surprise.

"You're early this morning. Are you helping Ava with her garden?"

Sophia explained.

Rainbow stamped a hoof. "I'll try to help," he said. "But that part of my magic only works if I am helping someone see something they desperately want to see—their heart's desire."

"I desperately want to see if there are any fruiting sky-berry bushes," said Ava.

"Me too," chimed in Sophia.

Rainbow tossed his mane. "Then here goes!"

He frowned in concentration. Sophia stood at his head, stroking his neck for support as he stamped his hoof sharply on the ground.

"Oh!" squeaked Ava as rainbow-colored sparks spun up into the air. She breathed the sweet scent in deeply. Burnt sugar, the smell of magic, was one of her favorite things.

The sparks became a disk of rainbow-colored

light spinning in the air. Inside the disk an image
began to form. Ava leaned forward, soaking up
every tiny detail. Sky-berry bushes, a thick cluster
of them. Ava studied the picture for clues to help
her find the bushes. There were shadows on the
ground, cast by the early-morning sun. "East,"
said Ava. "See the position of the sun? Those are
the eastern mountains."

There was a sharp *pop* and the ball of light exploded in a shower of glittering sparks. Ava blinked.

"We need more detail. The east is a huge area to search."

Rainbow hung his head. "I'm sorry, but without sky berries, I'm too tired to try again."

"Don't worry. You've done wonderfully," Sophia said, hugging him.

"We'd better tell Ms. Primrose." Ava wished she could ride Star back to school, but she'd already broken enough rules for one morning. She made a quick detour to Star's stable to explain what was happening and then left with Sophia, running like the wind, back to school.

Even though it was still early, Ms. Primrose was not in her bedroom.

"Let's try her office," Sophia suggested.

"Good thinking. She's probably up early

because she's worried too," said Ava, glancing at the tall wooden clock engraved with unicorns, ticking softly in the hallway.

"I can't wait to tell her what we saw," said Sophia as they hurried back downstairs.

Ava was out of breath by the time she reached Ms. Primrose's office. She raised her hand to knock and then realized the door was ajar and there were faint noises coming from inside.

"Ms. Primrose, please could we talk to you?" Pushing the door wider, she and Sophia stepped inside.

A bony figure was bent over the desk, going through one of the drawers.

"Ms. Nettles!" Ava and Sophia stared, mouths open.

Ms. Nettles slammed the drawer shut and swung around to face the girls, a furious look on her pointy face.

CHAPTER 7

"Out!" snapped Ms. Nettles, pointing at the door. "How dare you barge in here without knocking!" A red flush spread up her neck.

Ava and Sophia stumbled backward until they were in the doorway. Sophia knocked hesitantly on the open door. "Um . . . Ms. Nettles?"

"That's better." Regaining her composure, Ms. Nettles drew herself up to her full height. "Now, what is the meaning of you charging in here?"

Ava glanced at Sophia. "We . . . I . . . We thought . . ." She stopped and took a few calm breaths while she organized what she wanted to say. "There have to be sky berries somewhere in the mountains, so we asked Rainbow to use his magic to find them. And he did." As Ava grew in confidence the words came faster. "There are plenty of healthy sky-berry bushes growing on the mountains' slopes."

Ms. Nettles frowned. "Really?"

Just then there was a noise behind them, and Ms. Primrose came bustling along the corridor. "Goodness gracious me, what are you all doing in my office?"

"Um . . ." Ava shot a look at Sophia. "We were looking for you, Ms. Primrose."

"Well, come inside," said Ms. Primrose as Ava and Sophia parted to allow her into her room. "How can I help you, girls?"

Ava explained, finishing with, "Please can we search for the sky berries with our unicorns, Ms.

Primrose? If we find any, we'll come straight back and tell the teachers."

A strange look flickered for a second in Ms. Primrose's eyes. But it passed so quickly that Ava decided she must have imagined it because Ms. Primrose was now smiling her usual kindly smile again. "Oh, Ava, dear, that's very brave, but I simply can't allow it. The mountains are dangerous and too big for you to cover alone, even to look for sky berries."

"What if the whole school helped?" Sophia asked. "Then we could search a much larger area."

"I'm sorry, girls. It's completely out of the question." Ms. Primrose shook her head.

Ava couldn't help noticing the twig caught in Ms. Primrose's hair and the smear of dirt on her cheek. As serious as the situation was, it made her want to giggle. Whatever had their head teacher been doing to get so messy? *But of course,* she realized, *she must have been out hunting for sky berries!*

"Please let us go," she begged.

"Please, Ms. Primrose!" Sophia added. "We have to do *something*. The unicorns will grow weaker without sky berries, and who will guard Sparkle Lake then?"

Ms. Nettles cleared her throat, making Ava jump. She had almost forgotten the Geography

and Culture teacher was there. "Girls, while I admire your spirit, Ms. Primrose is right. It's far too dangerous to let you search the mountains, especially with your unicorns already in a weakened state. The mountains are treacherous, with many hidden dangers, including wild animals."

Ava frowned. She didn't mind facing danger, not if it meant saving Star, Rainbow, and all the other unicorns. "But—"

"Wait!" Ms. Primrose interrupted. She smiled kindly. "On second thought, I believe you are right. A whole-school search party is a good idea. Ms. Nettles can organize one. I have a few things to do this morning, but when I'm finished I'll join you on Sage."

Ava was so thrilled she almost hugged Ms. Primrose. She managed to contain herself, sending Sophia a triumphant smile instead.

Ms. Primrose checked her watch. "It's breakfast time now. Make sure you have a good one. You have a very long day ahead. Now, Ms. Nettles, let's talk about the details. . . ."

Shooing Ava and Sophia into the hall, she closed the door behind them. The girls high-fived before racing off to the dining hall.

Ava was too impatient to get started to eat much for breakfast. Luckily, once she explained the plan, almost everyone else felt the same way, and it wasn't long before the whole school was gathered at the stables.

As the students led their unicorns into the yard, Ms. Nettles, helped by Billy and Jack, gave out panniers to collect berries in.

"Get into pairs," cried Jack bossily. "You have to tell old nettle patch where you're going before you start."

Ava was pleased to see that Olivia had paired

with Layla, as she linked arms with Sophia. "We should search in the east," she said. "That's where Star's magic showed the healthy berry bushes."

Ms. Nettles, however, disagreed. "Ridiculous," she snorted when Ava and Sophia told her of their plans. "Sky-berry bushes like sunshine and are far more likely to grow in the west and south. Anyway, Ms. Primrose looked in the east yesterday just to make sure, and she didn't find any bushes there. Rainbow must have been mistaken. You really shouldn't have asked him to use his magic, girls. It was very irresponsible of you. I imagine he is suffering from a lack of berries in his diet and he'll be tired now. Stick to the areas I suggest, or you'll be wasting your time."

"Erm . . ." Ava's heart was telling her that Rainbow was right, but her head argued that Ms. Nettles was a teacher, and teachers were supposed to know everything. "All right," she agreed reluctantly.

They set off. When they got to the mountains, everyone split up into their pairs. Ava and Sophia looked high and low, but as the day wore on, they hadn't found a single berry and Ava grew quieter.

"What's up?" Sophia asked. "You've hardly said a word in the last twenty minutes." They'd stopped and dismounted to let Star and Rainbow drink from a multicolored stream. "And you've got your thinking face on."

"No, I haven't." Ava hastily smoothed out her expression. Her brother and sister sometimes teased her about her "thinking face," saying the wrinkles it gave her made her look like a little old lady.

"You have!" said Sophia. "So, what's up?"

"I think we're going the wrong way," Ava blurted out, and immediately she felt better. "Rainbow's vision was very clear. It showed sky-berry bushes in the east. I know Ms. Nettles said the bushes like sunshine, but the most important thing they need is fertile soil, and there's plenty in the east."

"So we go east," said Sophia.

"But Ms. Nettles said not to," said Ava.

Star looked thoughtfully at Ava. "I think you should trust your instincts. They're usually right."

Ava looked into Star's brown eyes. They were totally sincere. Star wasn't just being nice to make her feel good. "Okay, let's go east, then."

Sophia nodded. At first they made good progress. There were lots of tracks that crisscrossed the mountains. Star and Rainbow cantered happily along until they reached an area that was covered by creepers and brambles with patches of treacherous bog. The unicorns dropped back to a walk as they picked their way through the prickly stems that spread across the floor.

"The soil here must be great for plants," said Ava, ducking to avoid being snared by a runaway bramble. "Look at the size of those thorns."

"And those conkberries," said Sophia. "They're bigger than soccer balls." She looked around uneasily. "It's really creepy in here."

"Be careful, Star!" said Ava, as Star tripped over a thick vine.

"I'm trying," protested Star. "But the creepers are deliberately tripping me up."

Ava laughed. "They can't be doing that. . . ." She broke off with a gasp as a creeper snagged around her arm, almost pulling her from Star's back. She wrenched her arm free. "You're right!" she exclaimed. "These plants must be enchanted!"

The unicorns snorted in alarm, and the color drained from Sophia's face. "You mean someone's put a spell on the plants? Ouch!" she squeaked, as a creeper snatched at her long hair.

"Yes!" Ava exclaimed. "Someone must be trying to stop people from coming this way."

"Why would anyone do that?" said Star, stamping on a thin creeper as it started to curl around one of her fetlocks.

"I don't know," said Ava, frowning at the thought of someone enchanting the plants with dark magic. "But I vote we go on and find out!"

"I'm in!" Sophia's chin lifted in defiance as she slapped a creeper away from Rainbow.

"Us too," Star and Rainbow chorused.

The plants grew more unruly with every step, winding around the unicorns' legs and snatching at Ava's and Sophia's clothes. Ava's skin prickled with goose bumps. It was very eerie.

Suddenly Rainbow stumbled, falling hard onto his knees. Sophia squealed as she lost her balance and tumbled over his head. Ava gasped, but a purple bubble instantly formed around Sophia,

catching her and floating her gently to the ground. The island's magic always protected the unicorns' riders so they never hurt themselves on the rare occasions they fell off.

The bubble burst into glitter and dissolved. Sophia raced to Rainbow's side. He was struggling to his feet. "Rainbow! Are you okay?"

"No!" Rainbow said miserably, holding up one of his front legs. Ava caught her breath as she saw a nasty gash running across his knee.

"I'm hurt! I can't walk, Sophia!"

He buried his face against her chest. She hugged him tightly, her eyes meeting Ava's.

Ava felt as if icy water was trickling down her spine as the creepers around them inched closer. What were they going to do now?

CHAPTER 8

A bramble grabbed Sophia's arm. "Get off!" she cried, prying it away.

Ava dismounted. Brambles snagged at her feet, but she fought back, pulling them aside. "This is all my fault for suggesting we come this way!" she said, feeling guilty. "Does it hurt a lot, Rainbow?"

Rainbow nodded miserably.

"We should have brought a first-aid kit—bandages, stuff like that," Ava babbled, unable to stop talking. "What are we going to do? We're stuck here! We're—"

"Ava!" interrupted Star. "Calm down."

Ava stared at Star. "I'm panicking, aren't I?"

"Yes." Star nuzzled her shoulder. "Breathe and think."

Ava took a couple of deep breaths as Star went on. "There are lots of plants around. Is there anything here you could use to help Rainbow's leg?"

Ava frowned. Star was right. Lots of plants had healing properties. "Knitbone!" she realized. "That's what we need. My dad taught me how to mash the leaves into a healing paste. It's quick and easy and works like magic on wounds or broken bones." She glanced at Rainbow, who was sorrowfully holding his leg up. Now that she was thinking about plants, she felt much calmer. "If I find some and make a paste, we can use it to heal Rainbow's leg." She pulled off her soft purple hoodie, which had been ripped by the brambles.

"Here," she said, putting her finger in a tear and making it bigger. "Make a bandage out of this, Sophia, and tie it tightly to stop the bleeding while I find some knitbone."

"While *we* find some knitbone," Star corrected Ava. "I'm coming with you."

Ava gave Star a grateful hug, then they set off through the dense undergrowth. Ava was glad for Star's company. If anything, the plants were getting more aggressive, and it was hard work forcing a way between them. Gradually, though, the vegetation began to thin until finally the mountain slope opened onto a grassy meadow. The whole area was speckled with bushes that were bursting with dark-blue berries and small green plants with red buds. Ava recognized the plants instantly.

"Knitbone!" she said, breaking into a run. "And look, Star! Sky-berry bushes as well!" She swept her arm around, happiness filling her. "I was right! Rainbow's magic was telling us where to go!"

Ava's first thought was to pick some sky berries for Star to eat, but then she remembered Rainbow with his injured leg. Star could wait a little while longer. She plucked a handful of berries, stuffing them into her pocket, then sank to her knees in the middle of a patch of knitbone. Star brought her two flat stones, and Ava quickly ground the fishbone-shaped leaves into a thick green paste. She wrapped it in some more leaves. "That's it. Let's get back to the others now!"

Ava vaulted onto Star, and they cantered back to Sophia and Rainbow, Star leaping the creepers that tried to snare her as she passed.

Ava removed Rainbow's bandage and thickly spread the green paste over his leg.

"That's incredible!" Sophia said as the edges of the wound came together to heal. "How does it feel?"

"Good." Rainbow tentatively put his weight on the leg. "It's like a miracle."

"This is the real miracle!" Ava said with a grin. She pulled the sky berries from her pocket. "Look what else Star and I found!"

"Sky berries!" exclaimed Rainbow.

Sophia squealed. "You found some bushes, Ava?"

"Yes. There are loads, so eat as much as you want," Ava urged Star and Rainbow as she shared the berries with them.

"That feels so much better," said Rainbow as he gobbled them up.

"I feel stronger already!" Star agreed.

Ava and Star led them through the brambles to where the sky-berry bushes were growing.

"They're healthy-looking bushes," said Ava. "I'll take cuttings and try growing them nearer to the academy."

While Ava and Sophia filled their panniers with sky berries and cuttings, Rainbow and Star munched happily from the bushes.

"All done!" Ava said at last. "Let's go and show Ms. Nettles."

"Ava . . ."

Something in Sophia's voice made Ava look up. "Oh no!" she whispered in horror.

While the girls had been busy, something else had been busy too! A ring of bushes with needle-sharp thorns had started growing around them and their unicorns, trapping them in a circle.

"What's happening?" Ava said.

Rainbow whinnied in alarm.

"It's okay, Rainbow!" shouted Sophia, running over to him and vaulting on. "Jump over them! Quick!"

Rainbow leaped forward, galloped a few strides, and soared over the still-growing bushes.

"Come on, Ava!" Sophia shouted.

Ava started to run to Star, but a creeper caught her ankle and pulled her to the ground. The bushes grew even taller. The thorns reached up toward the sky, trapping Ava and Star, leaving them no way out.

"Ava!" Sophia yelled desperately from the other side.

"We're trapped. The bushes are too high to jump," Ava called, her heart pounding. She kicked a leg, trying to rid it of the creeper curling around her ankle, but the creeper slithered tighter

84

around her leg and body while growing in size. In seconds, Ava's arms were pinned to her chest as she lay on the floor.

"Help!" Ava choked out the words. Her face turned red as the creeper squeezed her tighter. She was suffocating! She struggled but the creeper was too strong, and as she fought it, its sharp thorns inched closer and closer to her face. . . .

CHAPTER 9

"I'm coming, Ava!" Star kicked away the brambles wrapped around her hooves and leaped at the creeper attacking Ava. She stamped on it and tried to break Ava free. Rainbow whinnied from the other side of the thorny wall, and Sophia shouted out Ava's name.

The creeper seemed indestructible. The harder Star trod on it, the tighter it squeezed. Ava began to feel faint. She locked eyes with Star, pleading silently for help.

"Let go of Ava right now!" snorted Star furiously. Steam curled from her nostrils, and she smashed the creeper with her hooves. Sparks crackled into the air. Star stamped harder, tossing her mane.

"Star!" croaked Ava. There was a strong smell of burnt sugar. Ava breathed it in and felt slightly revived. "It's your magic, Star!" she panted.

Star whinnied in surprise. "It is?"

"Yes!"

The creeper began to wind toward Ava's face again. Star stamped, and this time a fountain of glittery sparks rose in the air. Some landed on the creeper. With a *pop*, it doubled in size.

Ava squeaked as she disappeared into its thick folds.

"No, no, no!" said Star in horror. "I'm so clumsy! I didn't mean for that to happen!"

"Ava? What's going on?" yelled Sophia.

Ava knew Sophia and Rainbow couldn't help her. Only Star could save her now. Using all her strength, she pushed aside the coils of the creeper. "Star, you've found your magic. It *is* plant magic. You can make things bigger or"—she gasped— "smaller!"

"That was me?" Star stared at the enormous creeper. "It can't be! I can't do growing magic."

"You can," insisted Ava. "Trust me, Star. You can do plant magic. Only you need to reverse it, quickly. Make the creeper shrink!"

Star's eyes met hers. "Please," squeaked Ava as the creeper tightened further. "You can do this, Star."

"But I'm too clumsy! What if I make it bigger again by mistake?" protested Star.

"No, you're not," gasped Ava. "You're the best and smartest unicorn in the world!"

Their eyes met. Star hesitated, then she snorted, striking her hoof firmly on the ground. Purple, green, and gold sparks exploded around her.

"I've found my magic!" whinnied Star in delight. Arching her neck, she stamped her hooves. A continuous fountain of sparks rained over the creeper.

There was a loud *bang*, and the creeper *ping*ed

back like an elastic band and landed in a heap. It writhed and hissed as it shrank until, with one tremendous shudder, it fell still.

Ava was pale as ice and shaking violently as she slowly stood up. She staggered over to Star. "You saved me!" she said as she buried her head in Star's silky mane. "I knew you would."

Star nuzzled her. "I couldn't have done it without you. You made me believe in myself, but I almost killed you." Star's eyes widened as she remembered. "When that creeper doubled in size . . ."

Ava started to giggle in nervous relief. "I thought it was the end too." She hugged Star tightly. "I'm glad you worked out how to use your magic!"

"What's happening?" Sophia shouted frantically from the other side of the wall of thorny bushes.

"We're okay!" Ava called back. She looked at the bushes. "Use your magic, Star."

With a confident whinny, Star trotted to the bushes and stamped her hoof. As sparks rained down on the bushes, they shrank to a normal size. Ava leaped on Star's back, and she jumped over the top of them, landing beside Rainbow and Sophia.

"You're okay!" said Sophia in relief. "Rainbow and I were really worried."

"Your hair, Ava!" Rainbow said, staring.

"What do you mean . . . ?" Ava stopped to catch a lock of lilac hair that had fallen into her eyes. "Star," she breathed, holding it out. "We've bonded."

Star turned her head and stared at the lock of purple hair, the exact same shade as her mane. "Hooray! This is the best day of my life! Oh, Ava. You're my best friend ever!"

"For always!" cried Ava in delight. She bent down and hugged Star's neck.

Rainbow whinnied, and Sophia whooped. As Ava sat back up on Star, Sophia smiled. "I'm so glad you've bonded."

"Me too," said Ava, her eyes sparkling. "But now let's get these sky berries back!"

The girls galloped off across the mountain on their unicorns. It was a long way back to the others. They dodged bushes and trees, the unicorns going as fast as they dared.

"Whoa! What's that?" asked Sophia, pointing suddenly to one side.

There was an urgency in her voice that made Ava sit up straighter and look. As she did so, something came galloping out from behind a bush—a figure in a flowing black cloak, riding a tall unicorn. The figure raised a hand, there was a sharp crack, and a vine snaked out of a tree. It snatched at Ava's arms, trying to pluck her from Star's back.

"Oh, no you don't!" Star hit back, blasting the vine with a shower of golden sparks. The vine hissed and shriveled to a motionless tendril.

BANG! A bush suddenly exploded in their path.

Rainbow swerved, throwing Sophia onto his neck. She shrieked as she clung on.

The cloaked figure laughed and pointed at Star. A creeper rose up and curled around Star's legs. Star tripped, but her own magic was strong enough to shrivel the creeper. Ava urged Star on as magic sparked in all directions. Creepers whipped in the air, and bushes exploded. Star and Rainbow rode on, dodging enchanted branches and tendrils.

With a snort, Star sent a giant bramble arching toward the masked figure. It caught the rider's cloak as they swerved away. Ava heard the ripping of cloth. She craned forward as the rider, with a

gaping tear in the cloak, struggled to stay upright. The unicorn wheeled around to face Star and galloped straight at her.

"No!" Ava gasped as the tall unicorn thundered toward them.

CHAPTER 10

Star reared up and shook her mane. Yellow, gold, and green sparks spun out from the silky strands and rained down on the bramble bushes in front of the cloaked figure. Immediately, the bushes doubled in size. Star stamped her front hooves.

CRACK!

The bushes grew up across the mountainside, forming a thorny and impassable wall. Stuck on the other side, the figure shrieked in anger. Star sent one last burst of magic barreling into the bush. The bush immediately grew even higher.

"That's awesome, Star!" cried Ava.

Star gave a triumphant whicker and then galloped after Rainbow, catching up and racing alongside him as they headed down to where the rest of the school was still searching.

"Ava, Sophia! There you are!" As they approached the lower slopes, they saw Scarlett, Isabel, Olivia, and Layla riding toward them, waving. "We've been out looking for you!" Olivia called. "Ms. Nettles sent us to find you."

"We've got sky berries!" Ava called back.

The others cheered. "I knew you'd find some!" said Olivia, her eyes glowing. "Let's go and tell Ms. Nettles before she starts looking for you herself."

They galloped back to the academy.

Students and unicorns were milling about in the stable yard. "Where's Ms. Nettles?" Ava called.

"Dunno," said Billy, breaking away from the others. "What's up? You look like you just galloped through a hedge backward."

"We did. Long story," said Ava. "Help us get these sky berries into the feed room."

"You've got sky berries? From where?" Billy demanded.

"Sky berries?" called another student, overhearing.

"Yes!" said Sophia. "Help us share them with all the unicorns."

The rest of the students ran over to help.

Ava quickly retrieved the cuttings she'd taken. "I'm going to plant these near the stables," she called to Sophia. "With Star's plant magic, they could fruit immediately."

Watched by Sophia and Rainbow, Ava and Star found a patch of land and planted the sky-berry cuttings together. When the last cutting was in the ground, Ava stroked Star's neck. "Time for magic. You can do it, Star."

Star snorted happily and then blew out. Sparkles shot from her nose and landed on the cuttings. At once, they started to grow! Leaves and branches popped out until the cuttings were full-grown bushes, with juicy ripe berries ready for eating.

"Star, that's amazing," breathed Sophia.

"It's magic!" said Rainbow.

Ava gave a happy sigh and then hugged Star. "Well done!"

"Girls, what's going on? I can smell magic, and I expressly forbade any unicorn to . . ." Ms. Primrose rode up on Sage. Her hair was tangled and she'd scratched her cheek. "Oh . . . ," she said, stopping and staring. "Sky berries! New bushes full of berries! Where on earth did you find them?"

Ava fed sky berries to Sage as she recounted the adventure on the mountain.

"Well!" said Ms. Primrose finally. "You have been clever!"

Just then, Ms. Nettles rode up on her unicorn, Thyme, with the rest of Sapphire dorm. "Girls! You had me worried." Her eyes were dark and her hair was full of twigs. "You're very late back . . ." She broke off. "Sky berries!" she exclaimed. Her glasses slid down her nose in shock. "How . . . ? Where . . . ?"

Ms. Primrose smiled. "We have a plentiful

100

supply of sky berries again, all thanks to Ava and Sophia, Star and Rainbow. Once again, Unicorn Academy is indebted to the girls from Sapphire dorm—and their unicorns, of course. They've saved the day."

The rest of Sapphire dorm cheered.

"Go, Ava! Go, Sophia!" whooped Isabel.

"Well, this is a surprise," said Ms. Nettles, blinking. "Well done, girls. Now, I imagine you must all be very hungry."

"I'm starving!" said Scarlett.

A thin smile stretched across Ms. Nettles's lips as she turned to Ms. Primrose. "Should I order a picnic supper to have out here by the sky-berry bushes as a reward?"

"That's an excellent plan," said Ms. Primrose, her eyes sweeping over the girls and their unicorns.

Soon, the girls were sitting on blankets, enjoying a picnic of sandwiches, cakes, fruit, and rainbow punch. The unicorns grazed on the sky berries, their tails swishing contentedly. The setting sun sent red and gold streaks across the sky and the air was heavy with the scent of sweet night-jasmine, which Star had made flower around them.

"Ava's so smart," Sophia said, recounting their adventure to the others for the tenth time.

"It wasn't me, it was Star," said Ava, blushing.

"You healed Rainbow, and you helped Star to believe in herself so she was able to find her magic," said Olivia.

"I wonder who the cloaked person was," said Scarlett.

"It's really creepy that they attacked you," said Isabel with a shiver.

While the others chatted about their adventures, Ava got up and went over to Star. "I'm glad you discovered your magic," she whispered.

"Me too," said Star, nuzzling her dark hair. "You helped me believe I could."

"You helped me loads too," said Ava, thinking about her panic when Rainbow was injured.

"Knowing how to heal Rainbow's leg, that was incredible," said Star.

Ava felt a glow spread through her. "I suppose I am quite good at some things. Reading and writing is hard for me, but I know a lot of other useful stuff."

"You're also helpful and kind, and I wouldn't want anyone else as my best friend," Star told her.

"Good, because we're going to be best friends forever." Ava threw her arms around Star and hugged her, the unicorn's mane blending with Ava's lilac lock of hair.

They watched the sun sink in the sky. Ava felt like she was going to burst with happiness. Not only was there a new crop of sky berries for the unicorns, but she finally believed that she deserved to be at Unicorn Academy. Ava had brilliant friends and the best unicorn ever.

A shooting star suddenly appeared in the dusk. "Look!" said Ava to Star.

"It's beautiful," said Star. Resting their heads together, they watched as the star traced its glittering pathway across the darkening sky.

Isabel and Cloud are
finding it hard to get along.
Can a thrilling adventure along the coast
of Unicorn Island bring them together?

Read on for a peek at the next book
in the Unicorn Academy series!

Excerpt text copyright © 2018 by Julie Sykes and Linda Chapman. Excerpt illustrations copyright © 2018 by Lucy Truman. Published by Random House Children's Books, a division of Penguin Random House LLC, New York. Originally published in paperback by Nosy Crow Ltd, London, in 2018.

CHAPTER 1

"Try again." Isabel pointed at the bundle of twigs surrounded by stones. "You can do this, Cloud. And think what fun it would be to make a fire."

Cloud nuzzled her. "Okay, Isabel, I'll try again for you. But I'm almost certain that I don't have fire magic."

It was lunchtime at Unicorn Academy, and most students and their unicorns were lazing around together on the banks of Sparkle Lake, enjoying the summer sunshine. Isabel and her unicorn, Cloud, had sneaked away to a quieter part of the grounds.

"You don't know for sure." Isabel stroked Cloud's neck, tracing the pale-blue swirls on his white coat. "I think you just need to try harder."

All the unicorns on Unicorn Island were born with a special magic power, although they couldn't be sure when that power would be revealed. Isabel was desperate for Cloud to discover his magic.

Please let Cloud be like Blaze and have fire magic, she thought.

Blaze, Scarlett's unicorn, had been one of the first unicorns to discover her magic. Isabel was happy for Scarlett, her best friend, but she secretly hated the fact that Blaze had discovered her magic before Cloud.

Cloud stared intently at the pile of sticks. He lifted a hoof and struck the ground.

"Again!" instructed Isabel. "Do it again, harder. I'm sure there was a spark."

Cloud rapped the ground repeatedly. The noise made Isabel's ears ring, and the dusty earth made Cloud sneeze.

"Achoo!" Cloud couldn't stop sneezing. "Sorry, Isabel. I really can't make fire."

Isabel heaved a sigh. "Okay, well, maybe fire magic isn't your thing. Why don't you try turning invisible again? I'm sure the tip of your ear vanished the last time you tried."

Cloud shook his head. "No, it didn't, and I think

we should stop. My parents told me that magic can't be rushed. We both need to be patient."

Isabel buried her face in his silver-and-blue mane, trying to hide the frustration inside her. Cloud was lovely, he was sweet and kind, but Isabel couldn't help wondering if Ms. Primrose, the academy's head teacher, had made a mistake when she put them together. Ms. Primrose said that she paired students with the best unicorn for them, but patient Cloud wasn't anything like competitive Isabel.

Is he really the right unicorn for me? she thought. *Surely I should have a lively, more adventurous unicorn like Blaze.*

Like all the other first years, Isabel was ten years old and had started at Unicorn Academy back in January. The students spent at least a year at the school, getting to know their own special unicorn and learning how to become guardians of Unicorn Island. Their beautiful island was nourished by the magical multicolored water that flowed from the center of the earth and out through a fountain in Sparkle Lake in the grounds of Unicorn Academy. The water was then carried around the island by rivers and streams, and its magical properties helped people, animals, and plants to flourish.

Most students and unicorns only spent a year at Unicorn Academy, but some stayed longer. Ms. Primrose called them the lucky ones because they got extra time at the academy while their unicorns discovered their magic or bonded with their student. When a unicorn and student bonded, a lock of the student's hair turned the same color as their unicorn's mane.

"I need a rest," said Cloud. "Let's go back to the lake."

"Okay," said Isabel, vaulting onto his back.

She really hoped Cloud would discover his magic soon. She didn't think she could bear staying at Unicorn Academy another year, after all her friends had left!

They set off for Sparkle Lake. Isabel shaded her eyes from the dazzling sunshine as they drew nearer. She could see her friends from Sapphire dorm sitting exactly where she'd left them. The group was talking in whispers, casting glances at Sparkle Lake. Isabel had a feeling she knew what they were talking about.

"Someone's definitely trying to cause trouble," said Sophia as she threaded daisies together in a long chain. "Too many bad things have happened for it to be a coincidence." Sophia pushed her hair back over her shoulder. "There was the time the lake was polluted and the time when it froze over—"

"But who would try to harm the lake?"

interrupted Ava. "Everyone knows that nothing
on Unicorn Island can flourish without its magical
water." She had replaced the usual sprig of forget-
me-nots in her chin-length hair with a red rose.

"I don't know, but whoever it was tried to harm
our unicorns too," said Layla with a shiver. She

reached out to stroke her unicorn Dancer's nose. "Remember how they almost destroyed the sky-berry bushes?"

Sky berries grew on the mountains behind the school. They were the unicorns' favorite food, and more importantly, they were rich in the vitamins the unicorns needed to stay healthy.

"It's really scary," said Sophia. "I wish we could do something to help."

"I don't think we should worry," said Olivia. "Ms. Primrose has promised to catch the person responsible."

"What if she doesn't, though?" Ava shot back. "It's been weeks since the sky-berry bushes were targeted, and no one's been caught yet. I'm going to ask my parents if they know of any plants that might help protect the academy." Ava's parents had a plant nursery.

"Good idea," said Sophia.

★ ★ ★

"And I'm going to keep reading books in the library to find any spells of protection that might be useful," said Layla.

"I'll help you," offered Olivia. She glanced at Isabel. "Do you want to help too?"

Isabel shrugged. "Maybe." Isabel was lucky that she found studying easy and could be at the top of the class with hardly any effort. But Isabel much preferred to be outside with Cloud, trying to discover his magic or having adventures, than slaving over her work! "Do any of you know where Scarlett and Blaze are?" she asked, seeing that her best friend wasn't with the others.

"I saw them trotting away with Billy and Lightning," said Sophia. "But I don't know where they went."

"I'll go and find them," said Isabel. "See you later."

Isabel and Cloud rode around the grounds

until Cloud stopped. "Can you hear that? That's Scarlett's laugh."

Isabel listened to the distant cheers and shrieks of laughter coming from near the orchard. "That's definitely Scarlett," she agreed. "Clever Cloud. Let's find out what she's doing."

Cloud whinnied with pleasure at the praise and broke into a canter. As they neared the orchard, Isabel inhaled the rich smell of magic. It always reminded her of burnt sugar. A second later she saw a trail of flames burning brightly in the air, then she spotted Scarlett and Blaze cantering in loops around the trees.

Billy and his unicorn, Lightning, watched from nearby, encouraging Blaze to perform more tricks.

"Ladies and gentlemen, it is time to give you the circle of fire!" yelled Scarlett, her blond hair flying out behind her and a huge smile plastered on her face.

Blaze skidded to a halt and stamped a hoof. *Crack!* Sparks flared, and a large circle of flames hovered in the air before her.

"*Drrrrrrrrrr!*" Scarlett made the sound of a drum roll. The flames crackled and hissed. Blaze cantered forward and leaped neatly through the ring of fire.

Billy whooped, and Lightning stamped his hooves in approval.

"That's brilliant!" called Cloud.

Scarlett rode over, grinning. "Did you see that, Isabel? Blaze just jumped through—"

"A circle of fire," Isabel finished for her, feelings of jealousy curling in her tummy. "I know. I've seen you do that like a million times."

The smile dropped from Scarlett's face. "Oh," she said. "Well, we can try something else if you want."

Isabel felt guilty as she saw her friend's hurt face. Perhaps her words had been a bit harsh. "It's awesome that Blaze can do so much with her fire magic, but let's do something we can all join in with, like a race?"

"I'm in!" said Billy. "Race you back to the stables. Last one back is a dorky donkey!"

Billy and Lightning set off even before Billy had

finished speaking. Isabel leaned forward, shouting in Cloud's ear to urge him on. But Cloud wasn't the fastest unicorn, and there was no way he could catch Billy and Lightning or even Scarlett and Blaze unless . . .

"Take a shortcut through the picnic area. You can easily jump over the tables," whispered Isabel.

"You're joking?" panted Cloud. "Think of the trouble we'll be in if we're caught."

"Please, Cloud. I want to win!" begged Isabel.

Cloud hesitated and then suddenly swerved. "Okay. Just this once. For you."

Isabel laughed loudly, loving the rush of air on her face as Cloud galloped full speed toward the picnic tables.

"Hold tight," he whinnied as the first bench loomed closer.

Isabel hung on to his mane. Would such a huge leap help Cloud find his magic? What if he could fly? Isabel's fingers curled even tighter around Cloud's mane. The ground seemed a long way down. She told herself she wasn't scared. The special island magic would keep her safe, forming a purple bubble around her to float her to the ground if she fell. But that didn't stop Isabel's stomach from twisting into a knot as Cloud soared way above the bench, landing with a thump and kicking up a clump of turf. He jumped again, even higher this time, clearing the second table with ease and galloping on toward the stables.

Isabel was breathless with excitement as they pulled up. "That was amazing," she panted, quickly forgetting her fright. "We won by miles!"

Isabel waited for Scarlett, Blaze, Billy, and Lightning to reach the stables.

"Well done!" cried Scarlett as Blaze arrived just after Lightning. "You won!"

"Cheater!" said Billy bitterly.

"You didn't say we couldn't take a shortcut," said Isabel, shrugging. "We won fair and square."

"All right," said Billy, rolling his eyes. "But next time we'll beat you."

"We'll see," said Isabel, sliding from Cloud's back. "Thanks, Cloud." She patted his neck and suddenly felt happier. "You're the best unicorn!"

Cloud nuzzled her hand. "And you're my *best friend*, Isabel," he said back.

Cover art copyright © 2017 by Andrew Farley. Purrmaids® is a registered trademark of KIKIDOODLE LLC and is used under license from KIKIDOODLE LLC.

#1277

RHCBooks.com   RHCB